TABLE OF CONTENTS

CHAPTER 1

Something new at school

One Monday, the headteacher, Mr Nguyen, held an assembly. "Our school is starting a new recycling programme!" he announced.

"I hope that doesn't mean more homework," Ali whispered.

"Shh," Yasmin whispered back.

Mr Nguyen explained. "Factories can make new things out of old things we no longer need. That is recycling. It's one way to help clean up our planet."

He showed the students a symbol.

"This symbol means an item can be recycled. Starting tomorrow, the whole school will collect plastic and metal items for recycling."

"Hooray!" Yasmin said. "I want to help make the planet clean!"

"I just want lunch!" said Ali.

Emma yawned.

CHAPTER 2

A difficult job

The next day, there were big

green bins around the school.

"We're going to be the best

recyclers!" Yasmin said at lunch.

Emma peered into Yasmin's

lunch box.

"You brought parathas! Can I have one?" Emma asked.

"Of course!" Yasmin said.

"Can I try one?" Ali asked.

Yasmin handed him a piece of hers.

Ali took a big bite. "That's delicious! I would do anything for more of those!" he said.

Ali finished his lunch and headed for the bins.

"Don't forget to recycle!"

Yasmin said.

"Oh yeah," Ali said. He threw

his water bottle toward the bins.

"Two points!" he yelled.

But the bottle landed in the

blue rubbish bin, *not* the green

recycling bin.

"No points!" Yasmin called

after him. But Ali didn't hear her.

Mr Nguyen appeared.

"I need some helpers to sort the recycling," he said.

Yasmin stood up. "We'll help!"

Emma shook her head. "Sorry. I have to finish my maths."

"But the planet . . . ," Yasmin mumbled.

Didn't her friends want to help?

Yasmin stayed to help the headteacher. She was sad to see that many kids hadn't put things in the right bins. Plastic items were in the rubbish. Rubbish was in the recycling. It was a big mess!

The headteacher sighed. "The students need encouragement to recycle more. Maybe a party for the class that recycles the most?"

Yasmin thought about her friends at lunch. She smiled. "How about a paratha party? I could ask my mama to help!"

"Delicious idea, Yasmin!" Mr Nguyen said. "Let's go and call her together."

CHAPTER 3

A delicious prize

Yasmin's mama agreed to make parathas for the party. Yasmin couldn't wait to tell her friends in class!

"Let's make posters to let everyone know," suggested their teacher, Ms Alex.

"I'll help!" Emma said.

They got out felt tips and
paper. When they were done,
Yasmin asked Ali to help hang
the posters.

Ali held one up. "A paratha
party?" he said. "Now I *love*
recycling!"

Yasmin beamed.

Ms Alex's students brought recycling all week. Yasmin brought empty soap bottles. Emma brought tins her family had collected.

Ali brought in the biggest bag of all. Tins, jugs and all kinds of bottles!

"We can recycle them all. I looked for the symbol!" Ali said.

Soon the green bins were full.

On Friday, Mr Nguyen held another assembly.

"Great job recycling, children!" he said. "The winner is . . . Ms Alex's class!"

Everyone cheered.

That afternoon, Yasmin's mother and Nani delivered lots of parathas to Ms Alex's room for the party.

"Helping the planet is great!"

said Yasmin.

"So are parathas!" Ali said,

and he took a big bite.

Think about it, talk about it

- ❋ Does your school have a recycling programme? If not, write a letter to your headteacher asking if you could start one.

- ❋ What are some ways you help the environment at home? Some families recycle. Some families compost their food scraps. Some families try to reduce their use of gas and electricity. Make a list of the ways your family could help to keep the planet clean.

- ❋ Yasmin realized that a prize of her mother's parathas might help her friends recycle more. Why was it important that she and Mr Nguyen ask her mother for permission first?

Learn Urdu with Yasmin!

Yasmin's family speaks both English and Urdu. Urdu is a language from Pakistan. Maybe you already know some Urdu words!

baba father

hijab scarf covering the hair

jaan life; a sweet nickname for a loved one

kitaab book

lassi a yogurt drink

nana grandfather on mother's side

nani grandmother on mother's side

paratha buttery flatbread with layers

salaam hello

shukriya thank you

Pakistan fun facts

Yasmin and her family are proud of their Pakistani culture. Yasmin loves to share facts about Pakistan!

Pakistan is on the continent of Asia, with India on one side and Afghanistan on the other.

The word Pakistan means "land of the pure" in Urdu and Persian.

Many languages are spoken in Pakistan, including Urdu, English, Saraiki, Punjabi, Pashto, Sindhi and Balochi.

The word paratha means layers of cooked dough. Paratha is often served with butter, pickles or other toppings.

Pakistan started a programme called Clean Green Pakistan in 2018 to help improve the country's environment.

Make a recycle monster

SUPPLIES:

- 2 large brown paper bags
- felt tips
- scissors
- tape

STEPS:

1. Turn one paper bag up upside down. On the front, draw eyes, a nose and a big open mouth – big enough to fit bottles and cans through.

2. Cut out the mouth so there is an opening in the middle of the bag.

3. Lay down the second bag right side up and write FEED ME! on it.

4. Draw the recycle symbol underneath the words.

5. Place the first bag over the opening of the second and tape the two open sides together.

6. Place your Recycle Monster in your room, kitchen, or classroom and feed it recycling!

About the Author

Saadia Faruqi is a Pakistani American writer, interfaith activist and cultural sensitivity trainer featured in *O Magazine*. She is author of two children's novels, *A Place at the Table* and *A Thousand Questions*. She is also editor-in-chief of *Blue Minaret*, an online magazine of poetry, short stories and art. Besides writing books, she also loves reading, binge-watching her favourite shows and taking naps. She lives in Houston, Texas, USA, with her husband and children.

Hatem Aly is an Egyptian-born illustrator whose work has been published all over the world. He currently lives in beautiful New Brunswick, Canada, with his wife, son and more pets than people. When he is not dipping cookies in a cup of tea or staring at blank pieces of paper, he is usually drawing, reading or daydreaming. You can see his art in books that earned multiple starred reviews and positions on the *NYT* Best-Sellers list, such as *The Proudest Blue* (with Ibtihaj Muhammad & S.K. Ali) and *The Inquisitor's Tale* (with Adam Gidwitz), a Newbery Honor winner.

Join Yasmin on all her adventures!

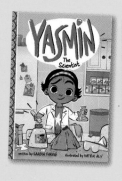  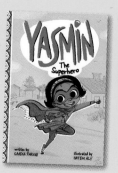 

 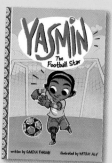 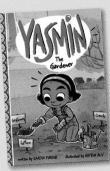 

 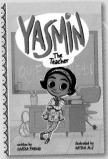 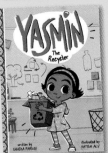 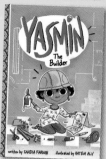